BENNY'S PENNIES

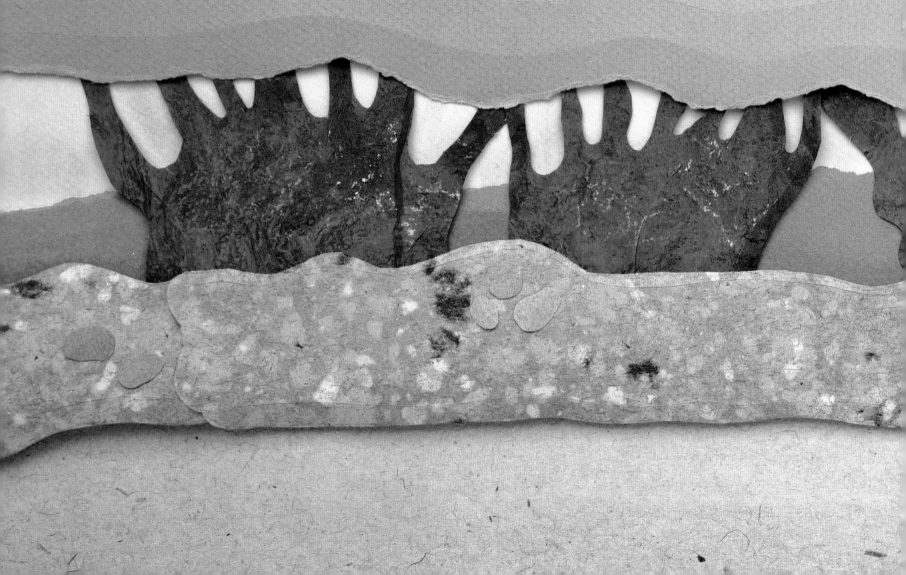

A PICTURE YEARLING BOOK

BENNY'S PENNIES

BY PAT BRISSON · ILLUSTRATED BY BOB BARNER

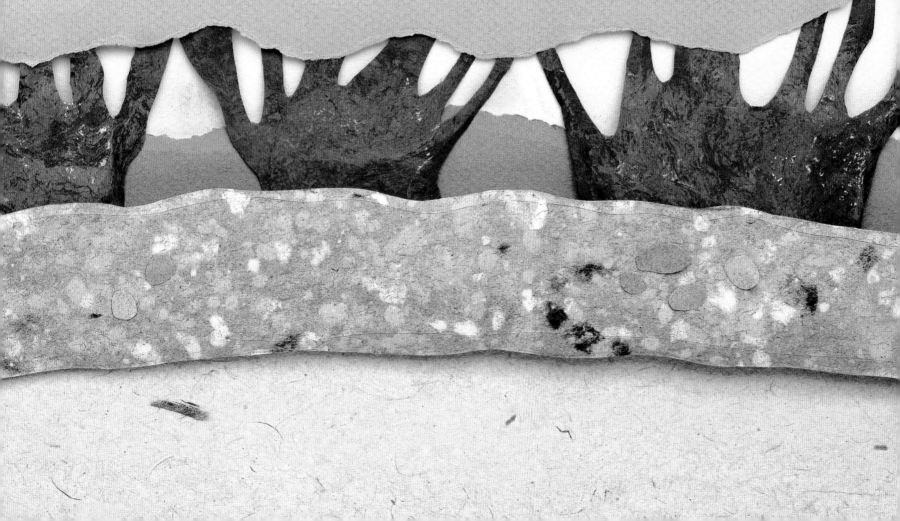

For my very own Benjamin Thomas Brisson.
With love, Mombo
P.B.

For Luddie
B.B.

Published by
Bantam Doubleday Dell Books for Young Readers
a division of
Bantam Doubleday Dell Publishing Group, Inc.
1540 Broadway
New York, New York 10036

ISBN: 0-440-41016-9

Reprinted by arrangement with Doubleday Books for Young Readers
Printed in the United States of America

August 1995
20 19 18 17 16 15 14 13 12 11

The illustrations for this book were created with torn and cut papers from Mexico, France, Japan, India, and the United States, pastels, colored pencils, various types of glue and paints. The text is set in 18 point Benguiat Book. Typography by Lynn Braswell.

Benny McBride had five new pennies.
"What should I buy?" he asked.

"Buy something beautiful," said his mom.
"Buy something good to eat," said his brother.

"Buy something nice to wear," said his sister.

"Woof! Woof!" said his dog.

"Meow!" said his cat.

"OK," Benny said. "I will."
So Benny McBride, with five new
pennies, strolled out in the morning sun.

A woman was cutting roses. Her name
was Mrs. Hill.

"Will you sell me a rose?" asked Benny.
"Will you sell me a rose for a penny?"
"Yes, I will," said Mrs. Hill.

Then Benny McBride, with four new
pennies and a sweet-smelling rose,
strolled on in the morning sun.

A girl was baking cookies.
Her name was Lucy May.

"Will you sell me a cookie?" asked Benny.
"Will you sell me a cookie for a penny?"
"A cookie for a penny? OK," said Lucy May.

Then Benny McBride, with three new pennies,
a sweet-smelling rose, and a soft warm
cookie, strolled on in the morning sun.

A boy was making hats.
His name was Michael Bess.

"Will you sell me a hat?" asked Benny.
"Will you sell me a hat for a penny?"
"Yes, oh yes," said Michael Bess.

Then Benny McBride, with two new
pennies, a sweet-smelling rose, a soft
warm cookie, and a fine paper hat,
strolled on in the morning sun.

A butcher was cutting meat. His name was Mr. Hopper.

"Will you sell me a bone?" asked Benny.
"Will you sell me a bone for a penny?"
"You're quite a shopper," said Mr. Hopper.

Then Benny McBride, with one new penny, a sweet-smelling rose, a soft warm cookie, a fine paper hat, and a big meaty bone, strolled on in the morning sun.

A man was catching fish. His name was Mr. Beal.

"Will you sell me a fish?" asked Benny.
"Will you sell me a fish for a penny?"
"It's a deal," said Mr. Beal.

Then Benny McBride, with a sweet-
smelling rose, a soft warm cookie, a fine
paper hat, a big meaty bone, a floppy
wet fish — but no new pennies — strolled
home in the morning sun.

"I'm back!" he called. "And I bought
what you said."

"It's beautiful!" said his mom.
"Mmm, good!" said his brother.
"I like it!" said his sister.
"Woof! Woof!" said his dog.
"Meow!" said his cat.

"Thank you, Benny!" they all said together.
"You're welcome," said Benny McBride.